My Little Book of

Wood Ducks

By Hope Irvin Marston
Illustrated by Maria Magdalena Brown

Windward Publishing
AN IMPRINT OF FINNEY COMPANY
www.finney-hobar.com

Two wood ducks flitted
in and out of the treetops at the
edge of the forest.

They were searching for
a safe place to make their nest.

SWISH!

The female
landed on a branch.

She squeezed into a
rotted woodpecker hole
in a big, old oak tree.

A gray squirrel that
once lived there had left a
bed of leaves.

The wood
duck sat down and
turned around. The
nest was just right.

She s-t-r-e-t-c-h-e-d
and fluffed her feathers.
As she preened herself, a
few downy feathers fell out.
The duck settled into her
new home.

Each day for nine days
the mother wood duck laid
one whitish egg in her nest.

She covered the eggs
with soft feathers to keep them
warm when she and her mate
were away. And to hide them
from hungry snakes.

One day the wood duck heard a strange sound.

scRITCH-scRATCH!

scRITCH-scRATCH!

scRITCH-scRATCH!

Something was climbing up her tree. She made sure her eggs were safely tucked beneath her. Then she peeked out. A raccoon was crawling up the trunk looking for lunch.

When he saw her, he backed down.

The next day while the wood ducks were feeding at the pond, the raccoon climbed the tree again.

He slipped away when he could not reach the eggs.

The mother duck sat on her nest for twenty-eight days. Inside the eggs, the ducklings began to grow. Their mother listened for sounds from the shells.

When she got hungry, she covered the eggs with down.

Then she flew to the pond to catch tadpoles, insects, and minnows with her mate.

On the thirtieth day, she heard a new sound.

"PEEP! PEEP!"

The first egg had hatched. Her waiting was over.

Crack!

Crack!

One by one the tiny wood ducks pipped their way out of their shells with their tiny beaks. Soon nine ducklings crowded the nest. Their mother kept them warm. In a few hours, the lively little babies were covered with fluffy down.

The next morning the mother duck flew down
to the ground.

"Tetetet!" she called softly. *"Tetetet!"*

Her babies heard her.

With their tiny claws, they scrambled up to the opening of the nest. Then they threw themselves out and dropped to the ground.

Their soft, downy coats kept them from getting hurt.

The nine little wood ducks trailed single file after their mother to the pond.

Suddenly a dark cloud
appeared above them.

It was a hawk.

"HOE-EEK! HOE-EEK!"

cried the mother duck. She and her babies scurried under cover to hide. Later, the wood duck hurried her ducklings to the water.

"Kuk, kuk, kuk, kuk, kuk," she called as she slid in. The ducklings waded in and swam after her. From now on, they would live on the pond.

The mother duck began teaching her babies how to catch insects. And tadpoles. And minnows.

"HOE-EEK! HOE-EEK!"

the mother duck called.

A snapping turtle was swimming toward the ducklings.

SPLASH!

Nine tiny ducklings dived and scattered. The turtle could not catch them.

When it was safe, the ducklings paddled back to their mother.

All morning they explored their new home.

Later the mother duck led them to the shore to rest.

One.

Two.

Three.

Four.

Five.

Six.

Seven.

Eight.

Nine.

Then the ducklings tucked their heads under their wings and went to sleep.

When they awakened, they were hungry. They pecked at the acorns and the beechnuts on the ground. Then they scooted back into the water.

**"HOE-EEK!
HOE-EEK!"**

A muskrat was heading
toward the ducklings. They
swam to shore and hid in the
undergrowth.

Soon the ducklings will lose their baby feathers and grow flying feathers.

One day they will fly away to build nests and start their own families.

But for now, they snuggle against their mother and go to sleep.

DEDICATIONS:

FOR KIM AND JEN-JEN
– H.I.M.

FOR ÉDES ANYÁM
– M.M.B.

Windward Publishing
3943 Meadowbrook Road
Minneapolis, MN 55426-4505
AN IMPRINT OF FINNEY COMPANY

www.finney-hobar.com

Printed in the United States of America